A Random House PICTUREBACK®

Hansel and Gretel

Hansel and

Illustrated by Sheilah Beckett

Retold by Linda Hayward

CDEFGHIJ 5 6 7 8 9 10 11 12 13 14 15 16 17 18 19 20

Gretel

Random House 🏠 New York

In a little house at the edge of a forest lived a poor woodcutter and his family. For a long time the woodcutter had not been able to find work. Without work, he had no money to buy food. His children, Hansel and Gretel, were always hungry.

The woodcutter had a wife who was very selfish. She was not the children's real mother and she did not care about them. Whenever there was a little food, she complained because she had to share it with Hansel and Gretel. Day after day she blamed her husband for being so poor.

The woodcutter did not know what to do. He was very troubled.

One night when they were all in bed, Hansel and Gretel heard the wife talking to their father.

"Listen," she said. "Tomorrow we will take the children into the forest and leave them there. Perhaps someone will find them and feed them."

Hansel and Gretel were afraid, but they kept very still until the wood-cutter and his wife went to sleep. At last Hansel thought of a plan. He put on his coat and tiptoed out the door. In the moonlight he could see many white pebbles in the yard. He stuffed them into his pockets and went back to bed.

Early the next morning the woodcutter's family went for a walk in the forest. As they hiked along, Hansel dropped the white pebbles on the ground. When they came to a berry patch, the wife told the children to pick berries until she and the woodcutter came back.

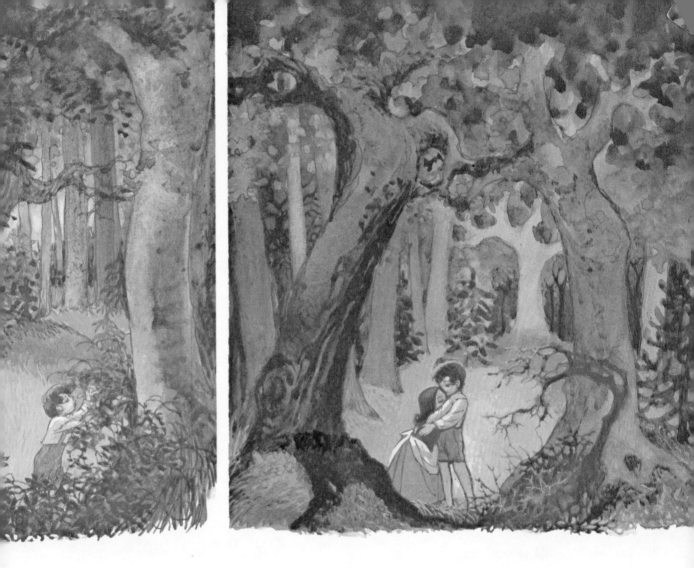

Many hours went by, but the woodcutter and his wife did not return. When it began to grow dark, Hansel and Gretel knew that they had been left in the forest.

"What will we do?" asked Gretel.

"Look!" said Hansel. "I made a path with white pebbles. We can see them in the moonlight and find our way home."

Hansel and Gretel followed the path of white pebbles through the forest until at last they saw the little house where they lived.

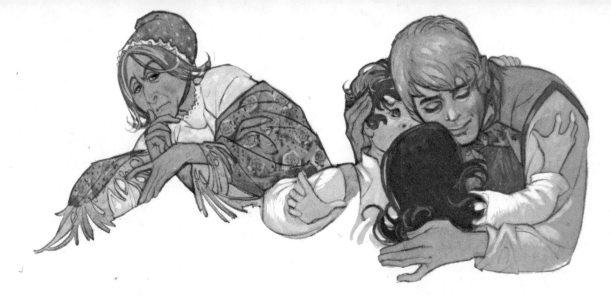

The woodcutter was very happy to see them, but his wife was furious.
The next morning she said they were going into the forest to pick
berries *again*. This time Hansel could not fill his pockets with pebbles.

But the woodcutter gave each of them a crust of bread to take along,
and the bread gave Hansel an idea.

As they walked through the forest, he broke off little bits of white bread and dropped them on the ground. He thought he was making another trail, but he did not see that the birds were eating the bread crumbs almost as quickly as they fell.

When the woodcutter's family came to a berry patch, the wife told the children to stay there until she and the woodcutter came back.

Many hours went by, but the woodcutter and his wife did not return.

When it began to grow dark, Hansel and Gretel knew that they had been left in the forest once again.

"I'm hungry," said Gretel. "Let's eat our bread."

"I don't have my bread," said Hansel. "I used it to make a path."

But when they looked around, they could not find any bread crumbs.

"Maybe the birds ate them," said Gretel.

"Of course!" said Hansel sadly. "I never thought of that."

Hansel and Gretel wandered through the forest the rest of the night,
searching for a way out. But the more they walked, the deeper into the
forest they went.

Just before morning Hansel and Gretel lay down on a patch of grass
and fell asleep. They were too tired to take one more step.

When they opened their eyes the sun was coming up, and they stared in astonishment at what they saw.

"Are we dreaming?" cried Hansel.

"We can't be dreaming," said Gretel. "It looks real enough to eat."

There before them, sparkling in the sunlight, was the most amazing little house. It was made of gingerbread and chocolate bars, with candy heart tiles and a pink frosting roof. Sugar drops and lollypops were growing on cooky trees.

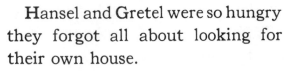

Hansel and Gretel were so hungry they forgot all about looking for their own house.

"If this is a house to eat," said Hansel, "then this is a house for us."

Hansel broke off a candy heart and Gretel nibbled on a candy cane. The gingerbread house was delicious.

Suddenly they heard a voice coming from inside.

"Nibble, nibble, like a mouse, Who's that nibbling at my house?"

The door creaked open and an old woman stuck her head out.

The old woman hobbled up to them. She was almost blind, so she had to lean very close to see their faces.

"My, my!" she said. "I do believe two little children are nibbling at my house.

"Now don't be afraid," said the old woman. "I won't hurt you."

Taking each of them by an arm, she led them into the little gingerbread house.

"Such a skinny boy!" said the old woman, squeezing Hansel's arm. "You need to eat. Sit down and I'll give you some breakfast. It won't take *me* long to put some fat on those bones."

She gave them huge plates full of fried apples and cornbread and sausages and pancakes. As they were eating, she heaped more and more food on their plates.

At last Hansel and Gretel put their heads down on the table and fell asleep.

"Ha! I've got them now," cackled the old woman. "Soon they will see what happens to little children who dare to nibble at *my* house."

The old woman had just pretended to be nice. She was really a mean old witch.

Suddenly she seized Hansel with her bony hand and snatched him out of his chair. His screams woke up Gretel.

"Leave my brother alone!" cried Gretel, tugging at the witch's skirt.

"Out of my way, you silly goose," screamed the witch.

She carried Hansel off to a little cage and locked him inside.

"It won't do you any good to scream, boy," she told him. "I must fatten you up. When you're nice and plump, you'll be a juicy supper for me.

"Stop your crying, girl," she told Gretel. "When the time comes, I will eat you, too. But first you can do some work for me."

Gretel did the witch's work.
She scrubbed the floors.

She cooked the food.

She washed the dishes.

And every night she took
Hansel his supper.

Every morning the old witch hobbled out to the cage and stuck her hand inside.

"Boy," she cried, "let me feel your arm. I want to know if you are fat enough to eat yet."

But Hansel knew that the witch did not see very well. So he held out a stick for her to feel.

The witch thought the stick was Hansel's arm.

"Why, you're not any fatter than you were yesterday," she cried. "I want a little meat on those bones before I eat you."

But finally she lost her patience.

"I can't wait any longer!" she cried. "Gretel, make me a fire. Fat or thin, your brother gets eaten today."

The old witch cackled with glee.

"A little bone, a little fat,
I'm hungry for a boy like that."

All the while she was making the fire, Gretel was trying to think of a way to save Hansel.

When the flames began to flare up, the witch asked, "Is the oven hot enough now?"

"No," said Gretel. "It is quite cold."

Soon the fire was blazing.

"*Now* is the oven hot enough?" asked the witch.

"How can I tell?" asked Gretel.

"Stick your head in, you senseless creature," said the witch. "And hurry up about it! I don't have all day."

"Will you show me how?" asked Gretel.

"What a stupid girl you are!" said the witch. "Here, watch me!"

The old woman hobbled over and stuck her head into the oven.

With one mighty shove, Gretel sent the wicked old witch flying head-first into the oven. She slammed the door and bolted it shut.

Then Gretel ran outside to open the cage.

"The old witch is dead!" she cried. "We are free, Hansel."

The two children began to run. They ran so fast, they never stopped to think about where they were going. They only wanted to be far, far away from that gingerbread house.

At last they came to the edge of the forest, and there before them was their own little house.

"Hansel! Gretel!" cried the woodcutter, as he rushed out the door. "You've come back!"

"Father! Father!" they shouted, as they raced into his arms.

Never before had Hansel and Gretel felt so happy to be home. The selfish wife had gone, and all their troubles seemed far away.

The little house at the edge of
the forest was full of happiness
again. The woodcutter was able to
find work, and Hansel and Gretel
helped with the chores.

Now and then the woodcutter
would take them in his arms and
say, "How lucky I am to have such
brave and clever children. I must
be the luckiest man alive!"